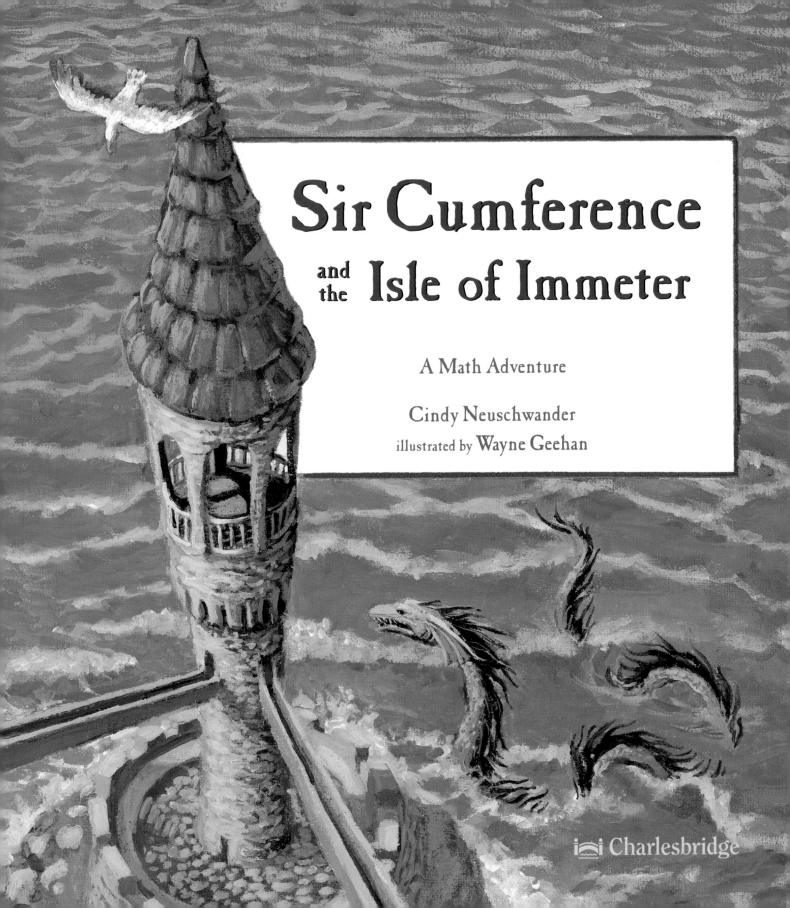

Sir Cumference
and the Isle of Immeter

A Math Adventure

Cindy Neuschwander
illustrated by Wayne Geehan

Charlesbridge

In memory of my dad, Max Grazda, who taught me the meaning of 110% — C. N.

For Greg Geehan and Alicja Modlinska . . . in search of their own Island — W. G.

Published by Charlesbridge, 85 Main Street, Watertown, MA 02472
(617) 926-0329 • www.charlesbridge.com

Library of Congress Cataloging-in-Publication Data

Neuschwander, Cindy.
  Sir Cumference and the Isle of Immeter / by Cindy Neuschwander ;
illustrated by Wayne Geehan.
     p. cm.
  ISBN-13: 978-1-57091-680-9; ISBN-10: 1-57091-680-2 (hardcover)
  ISBN-13: 978-1-57091-681-6; ISBN-10: 1-57091-681-0 (softcover)
  1. Geometry--Juvenile literature. I. Geehan, Wayne, ill. II. Title.
  QA445.5.N497 2006
  516--dc22

                        2005020747

Printed in Korea
(hc) 10 9 8 7 6 5 4 3 2   (sc) 10 9 8 7 6 5 4 3

Young Per sat with her uncle and aunt, Sir Cumference and Lady Di of Ameter. Her cousin Radius was teaching her the game of *Inners and Edges*.

"A player makes a shape out of tiles, calling out the number of squares used," explained Radius. "The first person to correctly count all the outside edges keeps those pieces."

Sir Cumference arranged his tiles into a square. "Inners are nine," he said.

"Twelve edges," counted Per, gathering up her winnings.

3

Lady Di made one long row of tiles. "Inners again are nine," she said.

"And edges are twenty!" exclaimed Per. "I love this game!"

"It belonged to the Countess Areana," said Sir Cumference. "She used to live on the Isle of Immeter, just off the coast. A sea serpent is said to guard the place now so no one dares to go there."

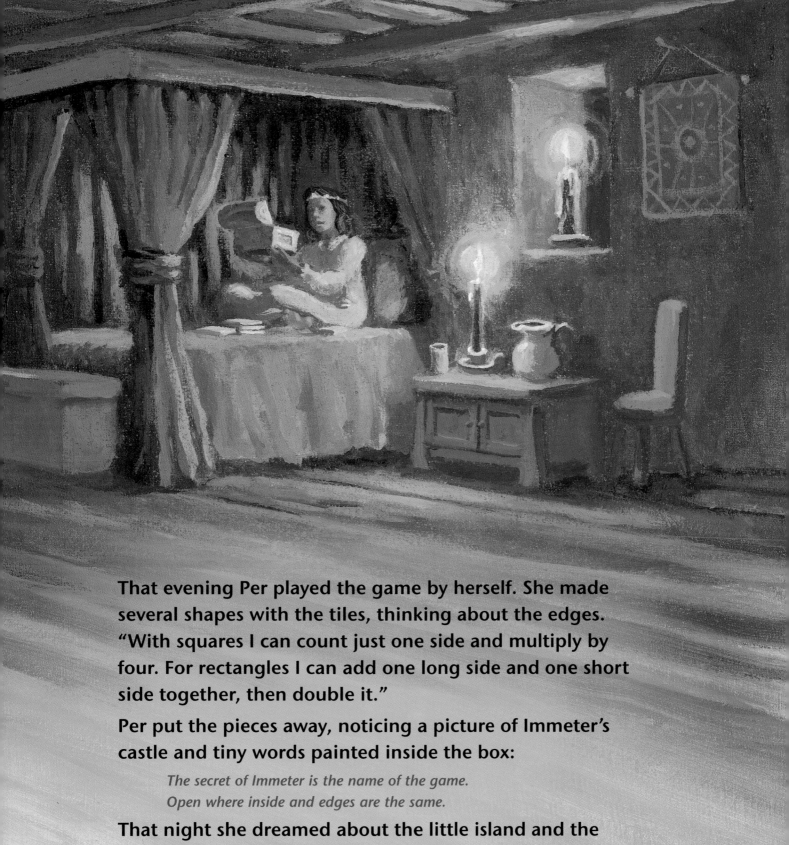

That evening Per played the game by herself. She made several shapes with the tiles, thinking about the edges. "With squares I can count just one side and multiply by four. For rectangles I can add one long side and one short side together, then double it."

Per put the pieces away, noticing a picture of Immeter's castle and tiny words painted inside the box:

The secret of Immeter is the name of the game.
Open where inside and edges are the same.

That night she dreamed about the little island and the mysterious message.

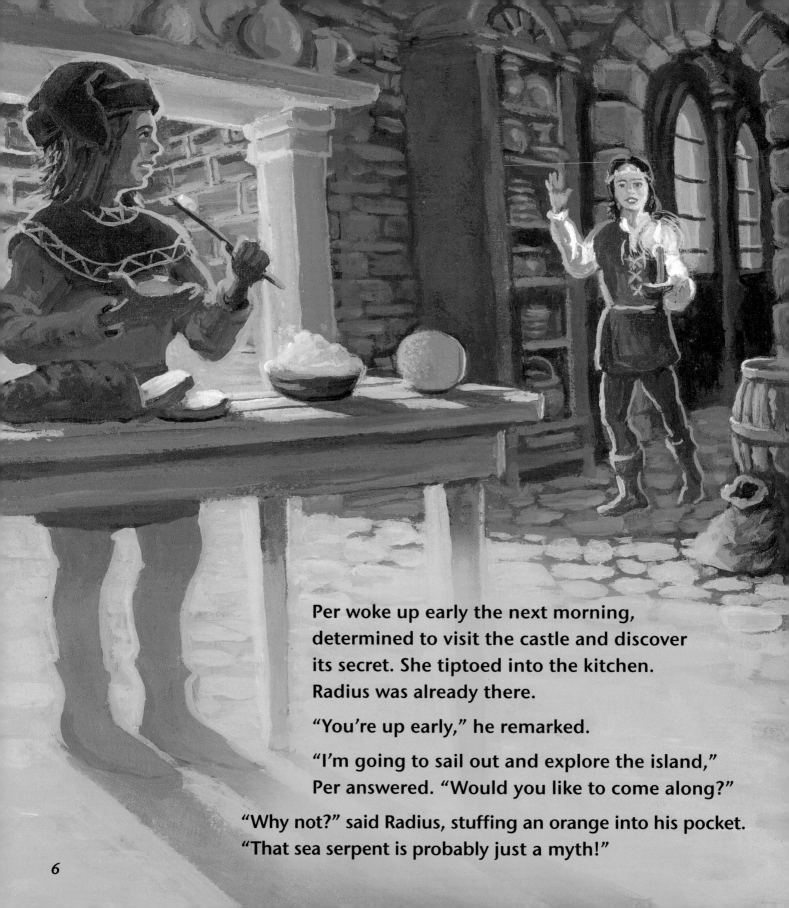

Per woke up early the next morning,
determined to visit the castle and discover
its secret. She tiptoed into the kitchen.
Radius was already there.

"You're up early," he remarked.

"I'm going to sail out and explore the island,"
Per answered. "Would you like to come along?"

"Why not?" said Radius, stuffing an orange into his pocket.
"That sea serpent is probably just a myth!"

6

Radius and Per hurried down to
the dock. They boarded a small sailboat
and headed for Immeter.

"We'll be there in no time with this breeze," said Radius.

When they reached the island, they walked around the castle. They counted seven walled-in doorways.

"These doorways remind me of a giant *Inners and Edges* game," said Per. "This one has 14 edges."

Radius nodded and said, "And 12 inners."

"That was fast," said Per.

"I multiplied the four stones down the side by the three stones across the top," answered Radius. "It's quicker than counting each one."

At the fifth doorway, Radius said, "Inners are sixteen."

"Edges are also sixteen," said Per.

"The inside and the outside are the same number," remarked Radius.

"The *Inners and Edges* box said, '*Open where inside and edges are the same*'!" exclaimed Per. "Could this be the entrance?"

She tapped on a stone and the door rumbled open.

The two cousins stepped inside just as large waves began crashing against the castle walls.

Per and Radius found themselves in a
hall with a grand stairway. They noticed
a large A in the middle of the floor.

"That A must stand for Areana," said Per.
"And look, there's a rhyme around the letter!"

Count half as many inside as out.
This unlocks the towers without a doubt.

"Count what?" Radius asked, gazing around the empty hall.

"How about these key shapes?" answered Per, looking at the floor. "Keys unlock towers."

11

Suddenly a window high above them shattered. In
snaked the head of a sea serpent! Its eyes glowed
green-gold and its scales shimmered like jewels.

"Quick! Let's start counting!" Per cried out as the
creature howled at them.

She pointed to the first key shape. "Twenty-eight edges!"

"Fifteen inners," said Radius. "That's not half as many inside as out!"

They tried another one. "Twenty-two edges!" cried Per.

"But only 10 inners," answered Radius.

Then Per found one with 24 outside edges.

"There are 12 squares inside! That equals half the edges!" cheered Radius. "This is the one!"

One of the tiles was loose. Radius lifted it up and saw a key. He grabbed it and they ran to the nearest tower.

They unlocked the door, ran inside and slammed it shut. "We're safe for now," gasped Per.

Radius looked at the ribbon tied to the key. "There are words on this," he said.

Where 200 floor squares fit inside,
Immeter's secret does reside.

"How can *square* tiles fit on the floor of a *round* room?" wondered Per.

Radius shrugged. "Right now, I'm too hungry to think."
He pulled the orange out of his pocket. He cut the fruit
and gave part to Per.

"This slice is round like the tower floor," she said.
She cut the piece into two halves. Then she stretched
the halves out and fit them together. "There! Now this
circle has been reshaped into a rectangle."

"A lumpy, bumpy rectangle," observed Radius.

So Per cut the eight orange segments equally into
sixteen smaller ones. These she rearranged into
a smoother rectangle.

"Much better," she said, "and we already know how to figure out the inside of this shape."

"Right," said Radius. "It's just like with the castle doorways. You multiply one long side by one short side."

"Halfway around the orange slice is the same as the long side," observed Per. "And the length of an orange segment is about the same as the short side. So we just multiply the two measurements to get the inners of the circle."

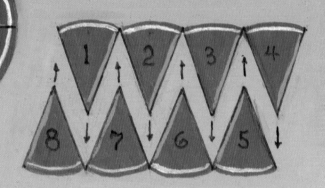

long side of rectangle = ½ circumference

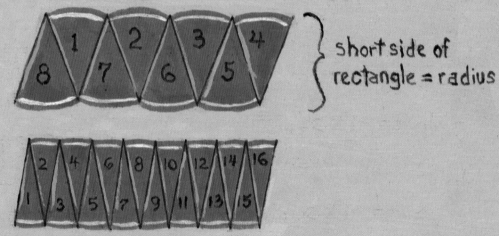

short side of rectangle = radius

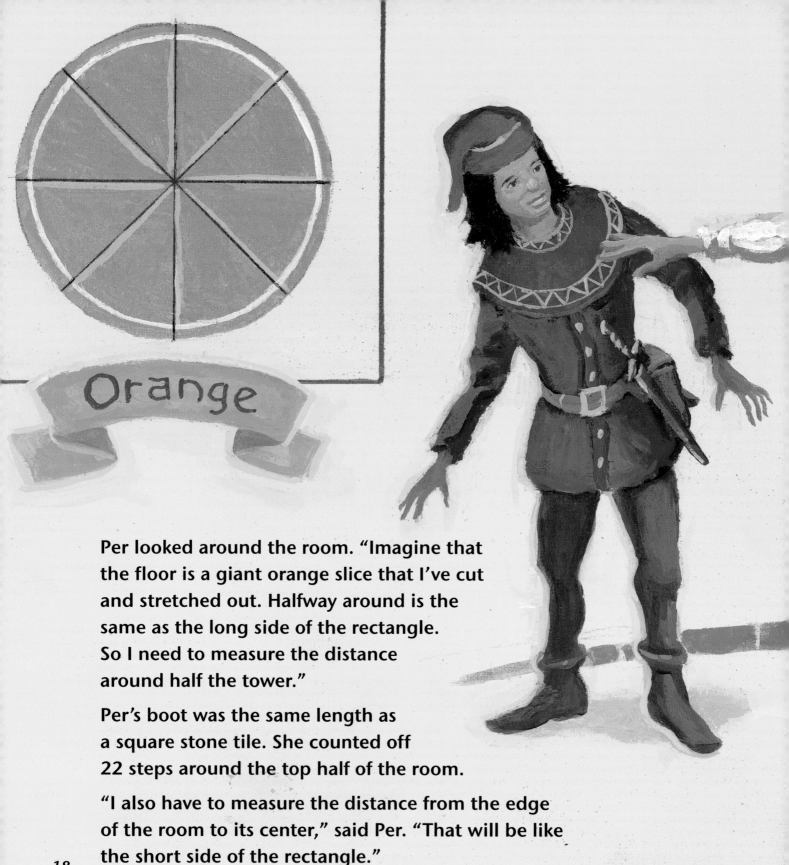

Orange

Per looked around the room. "Imagine that the floor is a giant orange slice that I've cut and stretched out. Halfway around is the same as the long side of the rectangle. So I need to measure the distance around half the tower."

Per's boot was the same length as a square stone tile. She counted off 22 steps around the top half of the room.

"I also have to measure the distance from the edge of the room to its center," said Per. "That will be like the short side of the rectangle."

Tower Floor

She stepped off seven squares.

Radius multiplied the two measurements.
"22 x 7 equals 154," he said.

"That's not enough," replied Per.
"We need to find a room with 200
floor squares. Let's keep looking."

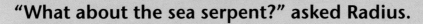

"What about the sea serpent?" asked Radius.

They cautiously opened the door. Everything was quiet.

"Let's go!" said Per.

Together they scrambled up a ladder and ran across a high walkway. Down below, the sea serpent erupted out of the water. Reaching up to grab them, it crashed into the stones. The walkway collapsed into the sea just as Radius and Per entered a second tower.

"That was a close call!" said Per, catching her breath.
They climbed up a spiral staircase. At the top, Per
and Radius found themselves in a bell tower.

"I don't think the sea serpent can reach us here,"
said Per.

"Let's hope not," answered Radius, peering over the edge.

21

Immediately Per counted off 25 boot lengths around half of the outside edge of the room. She then counted another eight steps from the edge to the floor's center.

"25 times 8 equals 200 squares!" she said. "This is the place! Now what do we do?"

Bell Tower Floor

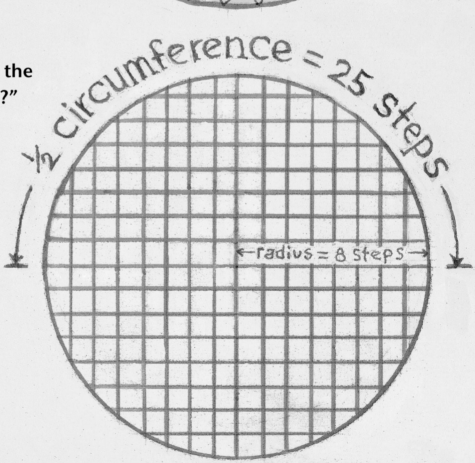

½ circumference = 25 steps

←radius = 8 steps→

"Look!" said Radius, pointing to words on the ceiling.

The squares in the circle are the secret's key. Use the number to signal the sea.

"This bell could be the signal," said Per, pulling on the rope.

Radius covered his ears and counted as Per rang it 200 times.

23

After the last peal, the ocean began churning and foaming. The monster rose up from the depths and faced Per. She stood before it, trying not to tremble. The creature's jaws opened and Per could see rows of gleaming teeth.

Out of its mouth dropped
a jeweled locket. Per caught it.
Inside was a note:

*The Isle of Immeter is yours to keep.
The Palimpsest will protect you awake
or asleep.*

The note was signed by
the Countess Areana.

"Are *you* the Palimpsest?"
Per asked the creature.

The sea serpent snorted
and bowed before her.

27

Radius and Per returned to the mainland riding on the
Palimpsest. Sir Cumference and Lady Di spotted them
from the castle and rushed down to greet them.

"Mercy upon us!" they exclaimed. "You're riding on
a sea serpent!"

"We've had an amazing adventure!" said Per.

"Tell us all about it!" said her uncle and aunt.

"We unlocked the secret of the castle!" said Radius.
"Per is now the rightful owner of the Isle of Immeter!"

"We had to find a round tower room that contained exactly 200 floor squares," added Per. "We discovered that if you multiply the distance halfway around a circle by the distance from its edge to the center, you'll know how many squares could fit inside it."

Sir Cumference smiled. "So one half of the circumference times the radius equals the inside of a circle. Wonderful!"

The next day, Sir Cumference and Lady Di held a special celebration for Per. People from miles around attended.

"On behalf of the Countess Areana, I pronounce you Lady Per of Immeter," said Sir Cumference. "This adventure has taken you full circle."

Per curtsied. "Thank you," she said. "I'm really good now at counting edges."

Sir Cumference laughed. "So you are! For this reason, the outside edge of any flat, straight-sided shape shall be called the *perimeter* after you."

"What should we call the inside of these shapes?" asked Lady Di.

"Let's call it *area*," suggested Per, "in honor of Countess Areana and her amazing floors." And everyone burst into a round of applause.

Endnote

In the story, Lady Per of Immeter used an orange slice to figure out the area of a circle. She reshaped the slice into a rectangle where one half of its circumference was the length, and the radius was its width. By playing the game of *Inners and Edges*, Per also learned that the area of a rectangle equals its length multiplied by its width (A = l x w).

Armed with these two ideas, Per discovered that the inside of a circle could be figured out by multiplying one half of the circumference by its radius. That could be written as A = ($\frac{1}{2}$ C) x r.

The standard formula for the area of a circle is $A = \pi r^2$. The following steps illustrate how to move from Per's formula to the standard one.

- The circumference (C) of a circle is equal to pi (π) multiplied by its diameter (d). $C = \pi d$
  (*See Sir Cumference and the Dragon of Pi.*)

- Since one diameter equals two radii (d = 2r), 2r can be substituted for d. $C = \pi 2r$

- Per used one half of the circumference of the orange for the length (πr) of her rectangle. $\frac{1}{2} C = \pi r$

- She used one side of an orange section as its width (r). Then she multiplied these two measurements to find its area (A). $A = \pi r \times r$

- Any number multiplied by itself is squared ($r \times r = r^2$).

- The standard formula for calculating the area of a circle is $A = \pi r^2$